The
Christmas Cup

The Christmas Cup

NANCY RUTH PATTERSON

ILLUSTRATED BY
LESLIE BOWMAN

ORCHARD BOOKS
A division of Franklin Watts, Inc.
NEW YORK

Orchard Books
387 Park Avenue South
New York, New York 10016

Orchard Books is a division of Franklin Watts, Inc.
Manufactured in the United States of America
Book design by Martha Rago

10 9 8 7 6 5 4 3 2 1

The text of this book is set in 13.5 pt. Horley Old Style Light

Library of Congress Cataloging-in-Publication Data
Patterson, Nancy Ruth.
    The Christmas cup / Nancy Ruth Patterson ; illustrated by Leslie Bowman.
        p.   cm.
    Summary: Eight-year-old Megan and her grandmother turn a worthless
old cup to good use by saving money in it to buy a gift for a special
person at Christmas.
    ISBN 0-531-05821-2.   ISBN 0-531-08421-3 (lib. bdg.)
    [1. Gifts—Fiction.   2. Christmas—Fiction.   3. Grandmothers—
Fiction.]   I. Bowman, Leslie, ill.   II. Title.
PZ7.P27814Ch   1989
[Fic]—dc19   88-29112
                                                                  CIP
                                                                  AC

The Christmas Cup is dedicated to my mother,

Willeyne McCune Clemens,

who gave me my first beginning,

and to my brother, Jack Hunter Patterson, Jr.,

who gave me another.

With special thanks, also, to Clay Turner, Katie McCabe,

Judi Coolidge, Bonnie Horne, and Pam Feinour,

who showed me how to begin yet again.

· NANCY RUTH PATTERSON ·

Contents

The
Christmas Cup

CHAPTER · 1

Ann Megan McCallie

Her name was Ann Megan McCallie, but nobody ever called her that.

Her brother Charlie called her Fang because the two front teeth that belonged in her mouth were buried in the side yard where Boo had hidden his beef bones.

Charlie, who was three years older, had told Megan that if someone buried a tooth deep in the soil and watered it every morning, a tooth tree would grow.

She had planted the two teeth six inches deep and sprinkled them with the watering can twice a day for a week. Mr. Taylor, the neighbor who always wore suspenders that matched his red hair, told Megan that teeth would not grow like that.

"Who ever heard of a tooth tree?" he said laughing. Charlie's friends, who were in on the joke, laughed, too.

Sometimes, her brother called her P.Q., short for Patchwork Quilt. That was because Doc Butler had taped a white gauze patch over her left eye to make her lazy right one grow stronger. "You're the first on the block to have your own patch," he had said as he patted the adhesive tape firmly in place over her eyebrow.

Megan, squinting with her one eye, had the feeling she'd be the last one on the block to have one, too.

The other people in their sprawling white house on Main Cross Street didn't call her Megan that summer. Her mother called her Meggie; her father called her Meg. Nannie, her grandmother, called her Little M. That was the name Ann Megan McCallie liked best of all.

It wasn't just the summer of the teeth that wouldn't sprout or the lazy eye that had to grow stronger before the third grade started in the fall. For Megan, her eighth summer was the summer of the Christmas Cup.

CHAPTER 2

Megan in Business

It all started with the lemonade stand.

The hot pavement scorched Megan's feet as she ran the two hundred and eighty-two giant steps from her front door to Dumphrey's Meat Market on Mount Air Square. She knew better than to go uptown barefooted, but the thought of having her own lemonade stand had made Megan forget everything else that day. She stood in line to pay for a dozen lemons (the biggest in the bin), a two-pound bag of sugar, and a box of flowery paper cups. The cement floor at Dumphrey's felt cool.

"You havin' a party or somethin', Megan?" Mr. Dumphrey asked, as she handed him three wadded-up dollar bills her grandmother had given her.

"Or somethin', I guess," Megan answered.

She couldn't just go around announcing to the whole world that she was setting up business for herself—at least not yet. Too many things could go wrong. Maybe her father wouldn't be able to find the wood he needed for the stand at the Livingston Lumber Yard. Or maybe Mama would change her mind about letting her use the old lemonade crock that had been in the family ever since there was a family. Or maybe Charlie wouldn't help her letter the butcher-paper sign.

That reminded Megan of something she'd almost forgotten.

"Could I have about this much butcher paper for my grandmother?" Mr. Dumphrey measured off a piece twice as long as Megan could stretch her arms and stuck it in the paper bag beside the sack of sugar and the lemons she'd picked out.

"When do you get that patch off?" Mr. Dumphrey asked as he counted out three quarters and two pennies change.

"By Christmas, I guess," said Megan. Nobody had told her that, but it sounded like it could be true. Good things always happened at Christmas.

"Don't really matter," Mr. Dumphrey said. "Everybody knows you can read faster with one eye than anybody else

around here can with two. You're smart, like your father."

That was the worst thing about being Ann Megan McCallie. Being smart—and having everybody in town know it. Everyone seemed to admire her father because he was smart, but the kids just called her "teacher's pet."

Megan hated it when the other kids called her that name. Nannie told her not to worry, that people only make fun of others when they are jealous. Her grandmother had said it one night last summer when they were washing the supper dishes. Megan still remembered the conversation.

"What's jealous?" Megan had asked. She liked learning new words.

"Jealous is when somebody else really wants something that you have," Nannie explained. "It's not a good thing to be."

"What do I have that somebody could be jealous of?" Megan asked. She had never thought about it before.

"A family that loves you, for starters," Nannie said. "Most people never know the kind of love you take for granted."

"How do you know they love me?" Megan was sure that they did, but she wanted Nannie to say it anyway.

"Well, your father always leaves the house wearing that tie

you picked out for him when your class went to the state capital." Megan had spent most of her shopping time deciding on the lime green tie with the state of Missouri embroidered on the front. Nannie knew Megan's father left it in the glove compartment every morning before he went to the office—country lawyers always wore blue. But he really had worn it last Thanksgiving and for Megan's birthday dinner, too.

"And whose mother made her a spider outfit for Halloween, complete with legs that moved? And whose mother didn't tell your father when you got your best Sunday school dress caught in the spokes of your two-wheeler? Even though she'd told you not five minutes before to take that dress off before you played? And who helped you wallpaper your clubhouse with covers from *American Girl* magazine?"

Megan nodded. Of course she remembered all those things. How could she forget them?

"Are you sure Charlie loves me, too?" Megan had asked.

"Does he carry around the arrowhead you gave him as his lucky piece? Did he stay home from a baseball game to go to your first piano recital? Did he run all the way home to tell us your tooth had been knocked loose in a game of Red Rover?"

Megan smiled. She had never told that it was her brother who had teased her into playing the game in the first place.

"Do *you* love me, Nannie?" Megan had asked.

"Little M, you ask the silliest questions sometimes," Nannie had said softly.

The clang of Mr. Dumphrey's cash register made Megan stop thinking about last summer and start thinking about today again. She left Mr. Dumphrey's and walked the long way home, on the edge of the grassy ditch that led from the square, past the chicken hatchery, in front of Doc Butler's two-room office, down the back alley and through the gate of the white picket fence to her family's backyard.

If her family saw her coming back from town barefooted, they'd be disappointed. That's what they always said when Megan had been less than her best self. The McCallie family didn't do things like going around without shoes. "You could step on a nail and have to get a tetanus shot," she'd heard at least half a hundred times. Or, "Think of all the children who don't have nice shoes to wear."

But Megan liked the way the grass tickled her feet.

She walked through the back door, careful not to let the door slam, found a pair of holey tennis shoes in the give-away pile in the pantry, and slipped them on before anybody could see her tar-crusted feet. Nannie saw her coming through the dining room door.

"You didn't wear those holey shoes uptown did you, Little M?" her grandmother asked. Megan knew from her smile that she already knew the answer to the question.

"No, I didn't," Megan answered truthfully. She changed the subject.

"Will you show me how much sugar to measure, and can I stand on the stool to get the ice cubes down?" Megan asked.

"Yes, I will," her grandmother said, "and yes, you *may*."

The sugar was measured. Ice floated in chunks on the top of the lemonade crock; wedges of lemon rested belly-up on the bottom. Her father had hammered the last board in place. Nannie had covered the rough edges with wide sections of checkered oilcloth. Charlie had tacked the "LEMONADE— 5¢ PER CUP—CUP INCLUDED" sign into place.

Ann Megan McCallie was in business.

CHAPTER 3

An Embarrassing Purchase

Normally there was not much traffic on Main Cross Street. There was not even that much traffic in all of Mount Air, Missouri.

But today was not a normal day. An auction of antiques had been advertised all week on the radio, and Megan knew that the auction was the perfect place to sell her lemonade.

Auctioneers had set up next door to Megan's house to sell all of Miss Gracie Holcomb's antiques to the highest bidder. People from as far away as Peno Creek had come to town to see what her things would bring.

"Why are they selling the furniture?" Megan asked her grandmother.

"Miss Gracie doesn't need furniture anymore," Nannie said. "She's in heaven now. Since she didn't leave any family to give it to, she decided to give her money to the Baptist church for the new pipe organ they've been wanting."

"Will they put her name on it so everyone will know who gave the organ, like they did with the new stained-glass Jesus window at our church?"

"I suppose they will, Megan. But having your name on a little brass plate isn't why a person gives. Shouldn't be, at least. It's the giving itself that's special."

People came in green sedans and pick-up trucks, their pockets lined with money from this year's corn crop or last year's pigs. A bearded Mennonite farmer tied his horse-drawn buggy to a telephone pole. Kids parked their bikes near the back alley. The crowd bought antiques and bric-a-brac. And they bought lemonade—ice cold—5¢ a cup—flowery eight-ounce paper cup included.

The auctioneer's hammer fell for the four-poster bed. "Cele-brated its hundredth birthday years ago," he promised.

It fell for the porcelain chocolate pot and twelve cups and saucers that matched it perfectly. It fell for the cut-glass cake stand, for the wooden milk churn, and for the black electric fan with its brass finger guards. It fell for the 1945 Plymouth two-door sedan. "It was only driven on Sundays by a little old lady," the auctioneer said.

The crowd thinned as the afternoon wore on, and only a few dozen spectators circled the last box of goods on the auctioneer's podium. A sewing basket with odd buttons and a wooden darning egg—that went for one dollar. The complete collection of Tommy Dorsey 78 rpm records—that went for two dollars. Then the auctioneer brought out a milkshake cup.

An old, dented, rusty, pint-sized tin milkshake cup.

Megan had seen one before when she ordered a vanilla shake at the Candy Kitchen Restaurant on the square.

"Who'll give me a dollar, a dollar, a dollar . . . ?"

No one raised a hand.

"How 'bout a quarter, a quarter, a quarter . . . ?"

No one.

"Make it a dime, a dime, a dime . . ."

The crowd began to move about, looking at what was left in the boxes yet to be sold.

"You'd have to pay me to carry it away," someone said as the auctioneer tried for a nickel. "It's just a piece of junk."

The milkshake cup looked lonely, standing there among its richer antique cousins.

Ann Megan McCallie had never in her whole life tried to stand out in a crowd. But suddenly, everyone was looking straight at her.

And all she had said was, "I'll give you five dollars."

She knew she had made that much from her lemonade. She had counted the money in her change box at least half a hundred times that afternoon and knew for sure it was somewhere between $5.04 and $5.24. It was hard to keep all the pennies straight with so many customers standing in line.

The auctioneer stopped in the middle of his "Give me a nickel, nickel, nick . . .

"Sold to the little girl at the lemonade stand for five dollars," he boomed.

Megan took the cup from the auctioneer's table to the cashier's stand and counted out exactly five dollars in nickels and pennies and dimes. Then she counted it out again to be sure she hadn't cheated anybody.

As soon as she had settled her bill, Megan saw Linda and Brenda Corey sitting underneath a tree watching the goings on. They were twins—co-head cheerleaders for the Mount Air Wildcats. People said they were the prettiest girls ever to walk the streets of Mount Air, except for Megan's mother, who was very beautiful, even if Megan had to say so herself. But her mother was nice. She wasn't so sure about Linda and Brenda Corey.

"What's that you bought, Megan?" Linda asked.

"It's a valuable antique," Megan said.

"It's a piece of junk," said Brenda. "You paid five dollars for a piece of real junk."

"You got cheated, kid," said Brenda. "Your family's gonna kill you when they find out you spent five dollars for a piece of junk."

"Won't kill me," Megan said. "It's my money. They let me do whatever I want with my money."

"And I guess what you wanted was to pay five dollars for a piece of junk nobody else even wanted for a nickel."

Megan took the cup, slipped it back into the newspaper wrapping the cashier had given her, and ran across the yard home. Boo nipped playfully at her heels, but Megan didn't stop to play with him. She was crying.

She had spent the whole afternoon selling lemonade, and all she had to show for it was twenty-four cents and an old, dented, rusty, pint-sized tin milkshake cup.

"What on earth is the matter with you, Little M?" That was Nannie.

The words tumbled out. "Five dollars and twenty-four cents. All gone except for a few pennies. Darned old milkshake cup. Linda and Brenda Corey. Piece of junk anyway."

"Well, Linda and Brenda Corey may be pretty, and they may even be smart," said Nannie. "But they don't know everything. Together you and I can make that old cup beautiful. Don't you worry about a thing. Let's go take down your lemonade stand before the auctioneers sell that, too."

CHAPTER · 4

The Christmas Cup

Nannie and Megan sat on the back steps, stringing green beans and putting little pieces in a bowl to soak, as they plotted the legend of the Christmas Cup. That was the new name for Megan's "antique" milkshake cup.

It was as easy as one, two, three.

One. They would squirrel away in the Christmas Cup all the nickels and dimes and quarters that were left over from their shopping trips to the square or that Megan could earn by doing odd jobs. They wouldn't tell anyone about it. They'd hide their secret savings account under the pink linen tablecloth under the colored wrapping paper under the box of picture postcards in the second drawer of the old chest in the pantry. Nobody could ever find it there.

Two. They'd keep a list on fine, white, blue-lined stationery of all the people who had been especially good to them that year. Family didn't count. When Thanksgiving came, they'd decide who on that list had meant the most to their lives, and they'd buy that person a special Christmas gift.

Three. They'd never tell that person—or anyone else—where the Christmas gift came from. It would be their secret forever.

Megan loved to wait until the house was quiet and sneak back to the pantry, pulling out the second drawer of the chest, digging under the tablecloth and wrapping paper, pulling out the white stationery to add another name to the list, or dropping some coins into the Christmas Cup. As the Christmas Cup filled, the list inched longer and longer. Doc Butler had made it twice by September. When he changed her patch, he pulled off the adhesive tape ever so carefully, not fast and painfully like the nurse had done. And he didn't fuss at Megan when she whimpered after her booster shot. "Quit crying or you'll scare away all the customers," was all he had said as

she cradled her face in his white starched coat that smelled of shots yet to be given. And best of all, he told her the patch would come off for good a few weeks after school started in the fall.

Megan never knew who would make the Christmas Cup list next. She was somewhat surprised when Miss Annie Gallagher made it.

Miss Annie lived in a white frame duplex right across the street from Megan's house. She was bird-like, caged between the black bars of her walker, her bony hands clutching the metal frame as she inched her way along.

"Her face is just like a prune, it's so wrinkly," Megan told Nannie when she saw Miss Annie sitting on her front-porch swing one morning.

"Miss Annie looked that way when she taught me Shakespeare forty years ago," Nannie said.

"Was she a good teacher?"

"The best. I've never heard anyone read Shakespeare better than Miss Annie did."

"What's Shakespeare?" Megan asked as she cocked her head to one side.

"A writer, Megan. William Shakespeare was a writer. He's still my favorite." Nannie kept on mixing the batter for the cloverleaf rolls.

"What did he write?" asked Megan.

"Poetry. Plays."

"Name a good one," Megan asked as she wrote her name with her finger on a scrap of dough her grandmother had handed her.

"*Hamlet. Macbeth. Othello.* He wrote too many to name right now."

"Why'd you like 'em so much?"

"That was before people had radios to listen to *Amos and Andy* or *Baby Snooks.* So families used to read together aloud. Plays always seem better when they're read aloud."

"Like when we put on the plays we make up in the garage?"

Megan remembered the stage curtain made from an old sheet and an audience of Boo and Nicodemus and all the other neighborhood pets that didn't scramble away fast enough.

"Sort of like that, Megan. We'd sit in a circle in the living room, and we'd draw lots for a part to read. Sometimes we'd ask Miss Annie to come across the street and read Shakespeare for us. That was always a real treat."

"You reckon she'd read for me?"

"Her eyes have failed her, Megan. She's too proud to let on, but she can hardly see a thing."

"Couldn't hurt to ask her to read for me, could it, Nannie? All she could say is no if she didn't want to."

"I guess it couldn't hurt to ask."

Megan knocked on the front door of Miss Annie's house. Through the lace curtains at the windows that framed the door, Megan saw the old woman inch her way to the front porch.

"Ann Megan McCallie. It's Ann Megan McCallie," Megan called out loudly.

"You don't have to shout. I can hear just fine," Miss Annie said as she opened the door.

"My grandmother said you could read real good."

"I taught Ruth senior English. She was the best student in my class, and she would never have said 'real good.' She'd have said, 'She reads really well.'"

Megan wasn't sure what to say next. Maybe she would say

something else wrong. Maybe she would say it too loudly or not loudly enough.

"Would you read for me?"

"What would you like me to read?"

"Nannie said you used to read a play called *Oh Fellow*. It's by Shakespeare," said Megan, feeling very smart.

"The play is *Othello*, and it *is* by Shakespeare." Miss Annie was smiling now. Like everything else she did, it took her a long time to get the corners of her mouth to turn up. But it was there, that smile, both corners. Not exactly like a Halloween pumpkin, but not bad for a ninety-three-year-old woman.

"I'm not sure you'd like *Othello*. Let's try *A Midsummer Night's Dream*. Would you get it from the bookshelf? Fourth book from the left on the middle shelf. Brown book with gold leaf on the side. Right next to *Othello*. My books are alphabetized, first by authors, then by the work."

Megan counted over four, pulled the dusty book from its shelfmates, and set it in Miss Annie's hands. She got close enough to smell the lilac talcum powder and the Listerine.

Miss Annie drew herself up. Her shoulders were too stooped to sit straight, but she sat almost straight. And she began to read. Thirty minutes straight. A different voice for each character. Megan wasn't always sure what the words meant, but she knew it was better than radio. Better than *The Wizard of Oz*. Better than anything.

Megan didn't have the heart to tell Miss Annie that she was reading the book with the pages upside down.

The next day, Megan carefully lettered Miss Annie's name on line twenty-three of the blue-lined white linen stationery.

CHAPTER 5

The Mennonite Mishap

Megan had never seen a Mennonite up close before. But she didn't have to see one to know that one was coming. She could hear him coming down Main Cross Street in his hooded buggy, his horse clip-clopping, clip-clopping on the pavement, swishing at the flies with its tail, dropping big clumps of manure right where the car tires would squish them as they traveled to town.

"Not even safe to walk in the streets anymore, if you know what I mean," a neighbor had said after the Mennonite's buggy had passed.

Mennonite men always wore blue shirts and dark suspenders, and their beards stopped where their shirts started. Most of them looked like the photographs of Great-grandfather McCallie that sat on Nannie's dresser. The women wore prim navy blue bonnets and old-timey dresses that trailed the streets.

Megan knew that Mennonites never drove cars or let their children go to school with the other kids in town. They would just come into town on Thursdays and then disappear to their farms for the rest of the week.

And that's all Megan knew about the Mennonites—until she met one face to face.

Willis Bailey was with her when it happened. He was the best-looking boy in her class, and he walked Megan home every day after school, even if she was teacher's pet. He said her house was right on his way home, but Megan knew for a fact that walking her home took him two and a half blocks out of the way.

It was a Thursday in October, and they were walking back to school after lunch. They were playing "Watch Out for the Bombs." That's what they called the piles of fresh manure left by the Mennonites' horses.

Willis heard the sound first—clip-clopping, clip-clopping

on the pavement. He pushed Megan down behind a forsythia bush.

"Let's play 'Bomb the Horses Back'," said Willis. "We can throw rocks at them."

"It's not good to hurt animals," Megan said, thinking of Boo. "How 'bout the buggy? You can't hurt a buggy."

Willis didn't wait for an answer. He handed Megan a couple of stones he'd picked up from the road, keeping the biggest ones for himself.

They both threw at the same time. Willis' rock hit the seat of the buggy where the driver was sitting. Megan saw hers spew up dust from the road. She hadn't even come close.

"A girl can't hit the broad side of a barn," Willis said. Willis grinned as Megan raised her eyebrow.

They followed the buggy, careful to hide behind the row of bushes. Willis threw again. Ping. Then Megan threw. Not a ping. A thud. Bull's-eye. Right on the rear of the buggy.

The man turned, showing no anger. His horse began jumping around in the harness, jerking the buggy sideways. "Whoah, now. Whoah. Whoah," said the driver.

Megan saw the buggy tilt, then start to roll along on two

wheels. A sack of flour spilled onto the ground. "Whoah, now. Whoah, girl," the man kept saying quietly to his horse.

"Let's get out of here," said Willis when he saw the buggy stagger, lean to one side, then fall.

"Whoah, now. Whoah," the man kept saying to the bay horse.

Megan and Willis raced across the square, past the statue of a town hero, past the First Farmers' Bank on the corner. They arrived at school just as class was starting after lunch.

"Not a bad aim for a girl," Willis said as they climbed the stairs to the second-floor classroom. "I didn't think you had it in you."

"I knew it all along."

CHAPTER 6

In the Principal's Office

The principal's name was Mabel J. Finney, and Megan remembered thinking that she had never heard anyone call her Mabel or even Miss Mabel. Just Miss Finney.

She wore her skirts longer than the other women in town did. Her hair sat high on the back of her head, wrapped around a bun that everyone knew was fake, and fastened neatly at the neck with thin hair pins. A small pink birthmark spotted her cheek.

"I bet chalk wouldn't dare squeak when she's in the room," Willis had said one day.

"Why, Boo stopped barking and ran off, tail between his legs, when she crossed his path last week," said Megan. It wasn't really true, of course, but it sounded like something that could have happened.

The very thought of going to Miss Finney's office made even the worst boys in the sixth grade sit up straight and keep their spitballs to themselves.

At recess, far away from the second-floor window of the principal's office, the third-grade girls would jump rope to a chant they had made up all by themselves.

> *"Old Miss Finney,*
> *Not worth a penny,*
> *Sat eating her curds and whey.*
> *Along came a spider*
> *And sat down beside her.*
> *It ruined the spider's whole day."*

But Miss Finney had never been hateful to Megan. She had given her the Good Citizenship Award for the second grade, a very good-looking blue ribbon and a book by Laura Ingalls Wilder, Megan's favorite writer before she had heard Shakespeare.

Miss Finney had smiled when she saw Megan play the role of the shepherd at the Presbyterian Christmas pageant last year, too. And she had come to Megan's first piano recital. Megan played "Jingle Bells" and "The Calico Cat Climbs up the Scales," two very beautiful songs if Megan had to say so herself.

But Megan didn't have to say so herself because Miss Finney said it, too.

The class was writing definitions for their spelling words when Megan saw Miss Finney coming down the hall. Normally, the sight of her made Megan sit up a little straighter and put her feet flat on the floor.

But the sight of her today made Megan start to tingle all over, and a knot chewed away at her stomach.

Megan was sitting by the door, and she could see Miss Finney walking from classroom to classroom. She was scowling.

A man was walking from classroom to classroom with her.

And it wasn't just any man. It was the same one whose buggy she and Willis had toppled over less than half an hour ago.

First, into Miss Greene's class.

"No, they are not in there," the man said.

Then into Mrs. Barrett's second grade.

"Not in there, either," he said, shaking his head from side to side.

Megan tried hard to bury herself in the speller. She didn't look up, but she could feel them coming into the classroom.

The room was quiet. Real quiet.

Until the man said, "That one." He pointed at Willis Bailey first. "And that one." He looked straight at Megan.

"Willis Bailey doesn't surprise me one bit," said Miss Finney. "But are you *sure* the girl with him was Ann Megan McCallie?"

"I'm sure," said the man.

Megan heard his boots click against the oiled oak floor as he walked down the hall toward his buggy.

"Willis. Ann Megan. I'd like to see you in my office. Now. Right this minute," Miss Finney said.

"It wasn't really Megan's fault," Willis volunteered as Miss Finney shut the door to her office. "It was my rock that hit the buggy. You know a girl can't hit the broad side of a barn."

"Were you throwing rocks at this buggy, Ann Megan?" Miss Finney asked.

Megan's heart was pounding so fast that she could feel it through her navy sweater. The words stumbled out before she had even thought about what she was saying.

"I was aiming at a b-b-b-bumblebee," she stuttered, "and I m-m-m-missed."

Willis couldn't help but laugh at her silly excuse. Miss Finney didn't smile at all.

"I want to give you both some time to think about what you've done," Miss Finney said sternly. "And I want you back in my office at eight o'clock tomorrow morning."

Miss Finney walked toward the window and looked out onto the playground.

Then she looked back at Megan.

"I'm going to teach *you* a lesson you'll *never* forget," she said.

CHAPTER · 7

The Secret

"What do you think she'll do to us?" Megan asked Willis on the way back to class from Miss Finney's office. Willis had been to the principal's office before. He knew about such things.

"It won't be as bad as getting stung by that bumblebee you were aiming at." Willis was grinning again. She knew he was just trying to cheer her up, but she didn't feel like smiling.

She didn't want to go back to class, but Megan figured she'd been in enough trouble for one day. "They'll be looking to see if we've been crying," Megan said to Willis. She was determined not to.

They had started a spelling bee by the time Megan got back to the room. Usually, a spelling bee was one of Megan's favorite things. But today, she let Mildred Harris win. Megan deliberately put one "l" in the word "intelligent" when she knew *any* self-respecting third grader would know better than to do that.

Willis walked her home after school.

"I'm not gonna tell my folks," he said. "Are you?"

"No. Not ever. Not as long as I live. Maybe even longer," said Megan. She knew they'd be disappointed in her.

Megan didn't eat much dinner that night. She took only one bite of a chicken leg, even though her mother said she could pick it up with her fingers. She made valleys in her mashed potatoes with the back of her fork and let the milk gravy run through the ridges like rivers. Even that wasn't fun.

Megan didn't sleep well, either. She listened for the phone to ring. It might be Miss Finney calling to tell her parents. It only rang once. Someone was calling her father about a town meeting.

She lay awake, thinking about what Miss Finney might do

tomorrow. Maybe she wouldn't let her go on the class trip to see Mark Twain's cave in Hannibal. Megan had been looking forward to that ever since second grade. Or maybe she wouldn't let her be hall monitor in the sixth grade. That was Megan's goal right now. Or maybe she'd make her stay in and write "I will not throw rocks at Mennonites" on her tablet until it got too cold for recess outside.

Or maybe she'd have to write her parents a letter and tell them what she'd done. Miss Finney had made Elizabeth Marshall do that when she heard her say a curse word in the hall.

Charlie had told her once that Miss Finney kept a spanking machine locked in her office closet for kids who were really bad. After she had found out about the tooth tree, Megan didn't believe any more of Charlie's stories. But maybe this one was true, and maybe *she* had been that bad.

Sometimes, Megan could talk herself out of being in trouble at home by saying she was really, really sorry and would never, ever do what she had done wrong again. She thought about saying that to Miss Finney, but she knew it wouldn't work.

At precisely eight o'clock, Megan knocked on the door to Miss Finney's office.

"Come in," Miss Finney said. It was the same tone of voice she'd used the day before.

"Have you thought about what you did?"

" 'Most all night," Megan said. She couldn't look Miss Finney in the eyes. She wondered where Willis was.

"What did you think about?"

" 'Bout how lucky I was that the horse wasn't hurt . . . or the man. 'Bout how I was lucky he was a nice man. He could have been real mean."

"And was there a bumblebee, Megan?" Miss Finney asked.

"No ma'am. I just made that up. I know that was wrong, too. My father says there's nothing he hates worse than a lie."

They were both quiet for a little while. Megan could hear the other children playing outside.

Then Miss Finney got up and walked toward the closet. Megan's heart started to race again.

Miss Finney opened the door slowly. It creaked. There was nothing inside but a raincoat and a black umbrella.

"I've told Willis to meet us at my car," Miss Finney said, putting on her raincoat. "We're taking a little trip."

Megan didn't ask where they were going. She was sure she knew. Miss Finney was taking her home to tell her mother in person. Or to her father's office. That would be worse.

Willis was already in Miss Finney's car. He had claimed the back seat. Megan got in beside Miss Finney.

They drove slowly around the square, right past her father's office. "Not stopping there," Megan said to herself, relieved.

They drove right past Willis's house and on past the McCallie house on Main Cross Street. They didn't stop there, either.

Right past the junction with its produce market and onto the blacktop road. Right past the corn cribs and silos and barbed wire fences and the goats playing by the creek.

They stopped at a white frame farmhouse. There were chickens in the yard.

"I want you to come with me," Miss Finney said.

Willis and Megan followed Miss Finney to the front porch. A woman in a dark blue skirt answered Miss Finney's knock.

"You've come early for your eggs," the woman said.

"Yes, Elizabeth. I've come early this week."

"I'll tell Joseph you're here," the woman said. "And I'll send Rachel and Isaac to fetch the eggs."

Megan looked through the open door into the Mennonite's house. The walls were white and plain. There were no pictures, not even a mirror. There were no cushiony sofas, only hard-backed chairs and a wooden table. The room smelled like soap. A big pot on the wood stove glistened.

"Mennonites don't believe in having electricity in their homes," Miss Finney said as if answering Megan's unasked question. "They live a simple life."

Joseph came up on the porch, wiping his hands on a piece of flour sack. "You've come early this week," he said. "The children will be here soon with your eggs."

Joseph looked like the man Megan had seen yesterday. Taller, but with the same kind of clothes and the same long beard and the same serious face.

"I don't see any tractors. Don't you use tractors?" Willis asked Joseph. Those were the first words Willis had said since they had left the school.

"We farm with horses and plows," said Joseph.

"Why?" Willis asked. Megan couldn't believe he was bold enough to ask. She expected Miss Finney to make him stop asking questions. Miss Finney let him go on.

"We have all we need," Joseph said. "Faith and family and farm—that is enough for any man."

"Do you like being a Mennonite?" Willis asked. "Don't you ever want to listen to the radio or go real fast down the highway in a car?" Megan couldn't believe what Willis was asking.

"We have what matters," Joseph said.

The children came with the eggs. Miss Finney paid for them in quarters and said she'd see them again next week.

As she left the porch, Megan noticed the doll Rachel was carrying. It was dressed like a Mennonite, but it had no face.

"What a person looks like doesn't matter to the Mennonites," Miss Finney said to Megan, as if answering her unasked question again. "It's the heart they care about."

The car was silent as Miss Finney drove back to school. Willis played with the lock on the door, making it go up and down until Miss Finney made him stop. Megan sat with her hands in her lap.

It was recess when they got back. "Can I play baseball?" Willis asked as the car rolled to a stop. Miss Finney told him to go finish the lessons he'd missed that morning.

Megan lingered in the car.

"I feel just horrible about what I did yesterday," Megan began. She wiped a tear that trickled from her eye to the end of her nose.

"I know you do, Megan," said Miss Finney.

"I thought I knew everything about Mennonites," said Megan. " 'Bout their horses and what they do to the street. 'Bout how they act outright strange, what with their beards and their buggies and their bonnets. How they hardly ever speak to anybody when they come to town."

"That's just their way, Ann Megan," said Miss Finney. "That's part of their religion, their faith. Like passing the communion plate or going in the baptismal water if you're Baptist."

"But nobody ever feels like throwing rocks at the people who go to our church," said Megan.

Miss Finney was smiling. "I bet people sometimes feel like

throwing rocks at Presbyterians," she said. "But Mennonites are easier to spot than Presbyterians."

Megan wasn't afraid of Miss Finney anymore. She was just ashamed. Ashamed of herself.

"What about my punishment?" Megan asked. She wanted to get it over with, whatever it was.

"Nothing I could do could make you feel any worse," Miss Finney said.

"I won't get the good citizenship award this year, will I, Miss Finney?"

"There's next year," said Miss Finney. "And lots of years after that."

"I want my family to be proud of me," Megan said.

"You'll make them proud," said Miss Finney. "You'll make them proud."

"You gonna tell my family?" Megan asked.

"Not if you don't want me to," Miss Finney said.

At that moment, Ann Megan McCallie couldn't think of one thing in the whole wide world she wanted any less.

"I'd rather have it be our secret," Megan said.

CHAPTER · 8

A Big Decision

Megan had worked hard to earn the money for the Christmas Cup. She had made potholders on her little loom and sold them to the neighbors for a dime apiece. That was her best money-maker. And she had picked up acorns out of her yard—a penny for ten. Her father hated the way they smothered the grass and went crunch under his feet. And she'd delivered advertisements about the sale on pork chops at the grocery store. Mr. Dumphrey had paid her seventy-five cents for that.

The nickels and dimes and quarters had piled up almost to the top of the Christmas Cup by Thanksgiving. The list of those "who have been especially good to us" had grown to three pages—front and back. The time was coming to decide who should get the present.

But first came the counting.

The good china plates were dried and put away in the corner cupboard. The leftover turkey was tucked away in waxed paper. The kitchen still smelled of turkey broth and sweet pumpkin meat.

"Is it time yet?" asked Megan.

"I think it's safe," said Nannie. "We'll put some fruitcakes on the dining room table to keep the men from coming back into the kitchen for snacks."

Megan penciled a "Do Not Enter" sign on the back of some shirt cardboard from the laundry and hung it on the closed kitchen door.

"That'll stop them," Megan said.

"Do you think that sign will stop them from trying to find out what we're up to?" Nannie asked.

"Well, if they ask us what we're up to, I'll just say three feet eleven inches," said Megan, proud of her joke.

"And I'll just say five feet and one half inch," said Nannie, laughing with her.

"You always laugh at my jokes," said Megan.

"I guess I always think they're funny," said Nannie.

"Remember when I was little and we made up that secret code in church when we were supposed to be listening to Reverend Mosser's sermon?"

Nannie remembered. "You mean when you squeezed my hand three times to say 'I love you.' And I squeezed yours four to say 'I love you best.'"

"Do you still love me best?" Megan asked.

"You ask such silly questions."

They sat at the kitchen table, putting the coins in piles, laughing when the tall stacks tumbled over, stacking them up again. Counting by 25¢ stacks, 103 of them to be exact, there was $25.75.

Almost a fortune.

"We'd better decide who's going to get the gift first," said Megan. "If we decide what to get first, we might get it all wrong. Wouldn't it be funny to see Doc Butler in a frilly housecoat or Miss Annie in a striped necktie?"

"You're right," Nannie agreed.

Figuring out who would get the Christmas gift was harder than counting out the little stacks of coins that kept falling down. The list was long, the becauses, bountiful. Megan could picture every candidate, remember every reason that prompted their naming.

"You get to choose," Nannie told Megan after the coins were counted. "It's your cup. It's only fair that you get to choose."

"But it was *your* idea, Nannie. The Christmas Cup was *your* idea. It was just a piece of junk when I bought it."

"Then if it's my idea, I guess I can choose anyone I like to make the decision. And I choose Ann Megan McCallie."

Megan thought about her decision for a long time, running her fingers up and down the list, stopping now and then at a name that caught her consideration.

"I think we ought to give it to Miss Finney," said Megan finally.

"I think that's a good idea, Little M," said Nannie. "But I've forgotten exactly why you put her name on the list in the first place."

"I never told you," Megan said. "It's a secret between Miss Finney and me."

Megan knew that her grandmother would understand all about keeping a secret.

CHAPTER · 9

Merry Christmas

The present was bought—a beautiful pink angora sweater with pearls on the collar. Size medium. "Wash with care" on the label. Megan had picked it out herself from a catalogue that a St. Louis store had sent through the mail. Nannie had the package shipped parcel post in care of the post office so that no one would wonder what they were up to if the mailman delivered it when they weren't at home.

They walked to the post office every day to see if the package had come.

And when it did, they took it right home to see what they had chosen.

The pink sweater was very beautiful, all wrapped in fine tissue paper and laid out in a gold foil box.

Together, they wrapped it in red shiny paper, Megan cutting the see-through tape into little slivers, Nannie making the green bow sit up just right.

They picked out a card with angels on it to go with the gift.

"You'll have to write on it," said Megan. "She might recognize my handwriting."

"We could write 'From someone who loves you,'" suggested Nannie.

"Too mushy," said Megan. "How about 'From someone who respects you'?"

"Who wants to be *respected* at Christmas time?" shrugged Nannie. "How about 'Merry Christmas'?"

They both knew those were exactly the right words to pen on the card.

"Sometimes the right thing to say is so simple," said Megan.

On Christmas Eve, Nannie and Megan walked to Miss Finney's house together. It was late, long after the Christmas tree lights had dimmed on the square. Long after the carolers

had retired to their homes. Long after the rest of the family had sunk into feather beds. Long after Boo had snuggled close to Charlie for the night-before-Christmas sleep.

Nannie had promised to wake Megan after Santa had come and gone. Megan had promised not to open her eyes until they were out of the living room. She squeezed her eyes shut tight as she crossed the room, but she could still picture the tree limbs that tickled the ceiling and the presents that covered the floor.

The Missouri wind whipped at their legs, even with leggings in place. They had pulled their coats snug around their necks. Their mufflers hid their faces, and their boots guarded against the snow that was falling.

They walked in the middle of the road. Not a single car passed them on their way to Miss Finney's house. The snow nobody had walked on yet glistened under a nearly full moon. Carefully they propped the box with the pink angora sweater in it against the door of Miss Finney's front porch. Then they hurried away.

When they returned home, they sneaked quietly in through the back door, tiptoeing through the bathroom with its tub standing on clawed feet and its little gas heater sputtering softly. They ended up in Megan's room in the back of the house.

"Will you lie down beside me until I go to sleep?" Megan whispered to her grandmother. She could hear her heart beat as she laid her head on the feather pillow.

"I'll just drop down beside you till you drift off," Nannie said.

"What do you think Miss Finney will say when she finds our present with no name on it?" Megan asked in whispers.

"Better be quiet now, or they'll know we've been up to something."

"What if the sweater doesn't fit?"

"It'll fit, Little M. I promise it will fit."

"What if she doesn't like pink? She almost always wears something dark."

"She will love it, I'm sure."

"You were right, Nannie. The giving itself *is* special."

"I thought you'd feel that way," Nannie said.

"I feel like we've already had Christmas, Nannie, and it hasn't even started yet."

"I know, Little M. I feel that way, too."

The last thing Megan remembered before she dozed off to sleep that night was four short squeezes on the palm of her right hand.